DINOSAUR
WORLD CUP

Keith Brumpton

ORCHARD BOOKS

This book is dedicated to

Alicia and Asun
¡HO*LA*!

ORCHARD BOOKS
96 Leonard Street, London EC2A 4RH
Orchard Books Australia
14 Mars Road, Lane Cove, NSW 2066
First published in Great Britain 1994
First paperback publication 1994
© Keith Brumpton 1994
The right of Keith Brumpton to be identified as the author of this work has been asserted by him
in accordance with the Copyright, Designs and Patents Act, 1988.
A C.I.P catalogue record for this book is available from the British Library.
Hardback 1 85213 380 5
Paperback 1 85213 775 4
Printed in Belgium

Meet Terry Triceratops.
Terry was the manager of Dinosaur
Forest F.C., who happened to be the
worst football team for many a mile.
No one could ever remember them winning
a match (but then again, dinosaurs
don't have very long memories!).
Terry was also the team's goalkeeper.

This is the team photo. They were just about to play a match against Jurassic Albion and nobody gave them much of a chance.

And unfortunately they were all proved right!

Jurassic Albion won the game by ten goals to nil. Terry bent down to pick the ball out of the net so many times that his back was aching!

Everyone on the team felt low. As low as a millipede doing the limbo.

"We need a new goalkeeper," muttered 'Hazza' Hadrosaur and the rest of the team nodded their heads. Poor Terry! And then to make things even worse, Jimmy Cetiosaur said that he didn't want to play any more!

That night Terry walked home.
It was a lonely walk.

What a disaster !!! Even the team are against me now.

I'm the only fan he's got left.

Where can I find a new goalie? They don't exactly grow on trees...

Just then Terry heard a rustling in the branches above him... It was a young Pteranodon playing 'catch' with a slippery fish.

Amazingly, she never seemed to drop the fish, no matter how high she threw it.

On seeing Terry, she clambered down from the tree. She gave a
croak and introduced herself.
"My name is Pteradonna and I'm the best goalkeeper in the world."
Terry looked at the little Pteranodon and wondered if he'd misheard.
"Just give me a go," she croaked. "Just ten minutes in goal."
Terry thought for a moment and then waved his tail.

The next evening, Pteradonna arrived, looking nervous. Terry introduced her to the rest of the team, then asked 'Hazza" Hadrosaur to take a few shots.

'Hazza' had a hot shot. It was as hot as a volcano. Terry felt a little bit sorry for the young keeper.

But really he needn't have worried...

Pteradonna wasn't just good, she was brilliant! She saved every shot that 'Hazza' struck and made it all look easy.

Because Pteradonna was playing in goal, Terry had to change
the positions of the rest of the team. Some of them weren't happy.
Dinosaurs don't like changes (unless they happen over millions of years).

During their next practice match, things didn't go too well. Team mates kept bumping into each other...

No one knew who was where or what was what. It was

Gradually, though, things began to get better. Dinosaur Forest won three games in a row, and their fans began to wonder if they would win the World Cup itself.

Anything's possible.

Terry made a good full-back with his tough armour and spiky tail.

Good tackle, Terry.

Oliver Diplodocus moved to centre-half and began to win everything in the air.

That's not fair!

He headed the ball so far it came down with snow on.

Brrr...

And now Archie Opterix was on the wing he could use his speed to run past opponents...

before crossing to 'Hazza' Hadrosaur to head home.

GOAL!

And of course they had the brilliant Pteradonna in goal.

Pteradonna had become quite a star and soon her picture began to appear in the local papers.

Terry was so nervous he could hardly sleep. The final was only two days away and he hadn't felt this excited since his Mum had given him a tasty bush for his birthday.

Meanwhile, on the other side of the island, Tyrannosaurus Hotspur had just finished training. Long teeth were gleaming by the light of the volcano; trees had been flattened. They were looking forward to playing against Terry's team in the final.

Their manager was certain that Tyrannosaurus Hotspur would win the World Cup. They were tougher than Dinosaur Forest. They were meaner. And just in case, he had a secret plan to make sure they couldn't lose.

The rest of the team laughed when they heard the plan. Tyrannosauruses are like that .... they don't mind a bit of cheating!

The morning of the Cup Final arrived. It was warm and sunny. Giant ferns waved in the breeze. Dragonflies buzzed to and fro.

Pteradonna was out for her morning flap. She swooped from tree to tree, gobbling up the odd insect (she never ate much on the morning of a big game).

Just as she was thinking about flying home, the young lizard heard a twig snap behind her. Something rustled among the giant ferns.

Pteradonna turned to see what was happening. There was no one about. Perhaps she was just feeling jumpy because of the big game. Suddenly she stepped on a piece of ground, the ground vanished beneath her feet and she felt herself falling.

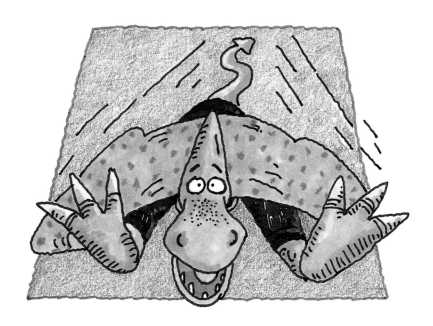

Pteradonna landed with a thump. Was she hurt? It seemed not, but she could feel a bump coming up on the crest at the back of her head. Everything went black...as black as a referee's shirt.
She looked up and saw two Tyrannosauruses standing above the hole into which she had fallen.

Pteradonna croaked out for the Tyrannosaurus players to let her go, but they had vanished back into the forest. Now she was all alone, and there seemed no way of escaping. The hole was too narrow to fly out of.

No one had seen the Tyrannosauruses carry out their plan. No one that is, except for a small Iguanodon called Ron. As luck would have it, Ron was a fan of Dinosaur Forest F.C. A big fan. The forest was empty except for the drone of dragonflies and the occasional rumble of a distant volcano.

There were just two hours to kick off. The fans were excited.

But Terry was worried. So worried he could hardly eat his ferns.
"What's up boss?" asked Cyril Stegosaurus.

"It's Pteradonna. No one has seen her since this morning. If she doesn't turn up we're bound to lose the game."

The rest of the team looked grim.

Pteradonna was never late. Where could she be?

"There's nothing for it," announced Terry.
"I'll have to go and look for her. I know a
spot in the forest where she usually trains."

But boss, that part of the forest is full of
Tyrannosauruses! They'll have you for supper!

"That's a chance I'll have to take.
If I don't make it back, 'Hazza'
takes over as captain."

And with that, he ran off
into the forest.

Terry knew time was short.
He crashed through bushes...

He swam across swamps...

He even climbed a tree to
try and get a better view.

'Who'd be a manager?' thought Terry, arriving at a part of the forest he'd never seen before. It was then that he heard in the distance the unmistakable call of a Pteranodon.

It didn't take long to find the trap into which poor Pteradonna had fallen. Terry told her to stay calm while he went for help. Luckily he met Ron Iguanodon, passing by on his way to the game...

Pteradonna could do nothing but wait to see if Terry and Ron could free her from the hole.

D'you think we'll make it in time for the game, boss?

Terry wasn't sure. Maybe there was still a chance - providing his plan worked. Claws crossed!

Grab this and we'll have you out in a jiffy!

"We'd better fly," gasped Pteradonna. "Er, I can't fly," replied Terry. "You go on ahead. I'll follow as quickly as I can." Pteradonna knew of a short-cut through the forest and showed Terry. "Good luck!"

Pteradonna flapped as fast as a Pteranodon can flap!

15 minutes to go...

10...

Terry ran as fast as a Triceratops can run!

5 minutes left...

2 minutes...

With just seconds to go, Pteradonna and Terry arrived. The rest of the team leapt for joy. The referee blew his nose to start the game.

Their plans in ruins, Tyrannosaurus Hotspur tried every trick they knew to stop Dinosaur Forest.

They threatened the ref...

They cheated...

They played with four huge defenders, taller than the goalposts.

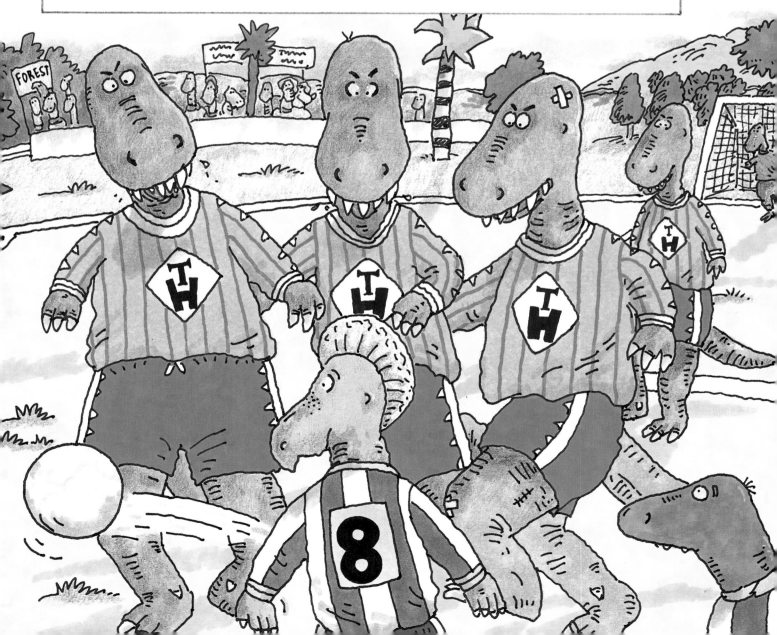

Terry actually felt quite relieved when half-time arrived and the score was still 0-0.

"We've got every chance to win this game," he said, when they were under their dressing tree.
"We're much fitter than they are. Remember Tyrannosauruses don't like running...Let's use our nippy forwards as much as possible."

The second half started with a smart save by Pteradonna...

She threw the ball to Archie...   who went on a great run..

The Tyrannosaurus team were getting tired just as Terry had said they would.

I need a chair.

With the crowd cheering him on, Archie crossed the ball, it hung in the air, and WHACK!
'Hazza' made the score one-nil!

Minutes later...

'Hazza' scored another brilliant goal!

WHUMF!!!

We can do it after all!

allez FOREST

FO-REST! FO-REST!

Tyrannosaurus Hotspur were now a beaten team. Their huge tails hung down beneath their legs. It was no surprise to anyone when Archie Opterix made it three-nil.

Pteradonna made some more great saves...

THUMP!

And Terry scored his first goal of the season - with his tail!

The World Cup belonged to Terry and his team!

Dinosaur Forest F.C.
v
Tyrannosaurus Hotspur

Cup Final Official Programme

 Dinosaur Forest F.C.

CLUB FACTS AND FIGURES

Full name: Dinosaur Forest F.C.
Founded: 150 million years ago.
Team colours: Blue and white striped shirts, blue shorts with yellow and red trim.
Away colours: Red Shirts, black shorts
Trophies won: None
Promoted: Never
Biggest Victory: 2-0 v. Dinosaur Forest Reserves
Biggest defeat: 0 - 19 v. Megadon Villa
Record attendance: 2

Manager: Terry Triceratops

 Tyrannosaurus Hotspur F.C.

CLUB FACTS AND FIGURES

Full name: Tyrannosaurus Hotspur
Founded: 180 million years ago
Team colours: White shirts, red shorts with black and white trim.
Away colours: Pink shirts, red shorts.
Trophies won: Dinosaur League
(8 times),
Inter-Swamp Trophy (4 times), Bad Behaviour Cup (42 times)
Biggest victory: 24-0 v. Iguanodon Hove Albion

Manager: Vinny Bones

STAR PLAYER

This week's star player is our popular young goalkeeper, Pteradonna. Since joining us from a tree in the forest, she has played in every game and helped us to our first ever cup final.

1. Pteradonna. Young goalkeeper with more clean sheets than a laundry. Trains by catching slippery fish.

2. Cyril Stegosaurus. Slow but solid defender. Rarely leaves his regular spot.

3. Steggy Stegoceras. Hard headed, powerful defender, has an extra strong skull.

4. Oliver Diplodocus. Great in the air and at corners where he can use his height.

5. Terry Triceratops. Captain and Manager, Terry likes to use his horns in the tackle.

6. Corynthia Corythosaurus. An adventurous player who likes to take people on. Corynthia dribbles a lot, especially in her own area. Likes wet pitches.

7. Eric Allosaurus. A powerful midfield player who is always hungry for the ball. Known to fight his brother, Albert, if things go badly.

8. Albert Allosaurus. Twin brother of Eric, and his partner in midfield. Very dangerous at set pieces and after the game if the team has lost.

10. Celia Coelophysis A tall, graceful forward who likes to run quickly at defences.

9. Howard 'Hazza' Hadrosaur. Top goalscorer last season.

11. Archie Opterix. Played at full back last season, but now prefers to stay on the wing. Tricky player, but flaps under pressure.